STEAK IT OR LEAVE IT

IRON & FLAME COZY MYSTERIES, BOOK 8

PATTI BENNING

SUMMER PRESCOTT BOOKS PUBLISHING

Copyright 2024 Summer Prescott Books

All Rights Reserved. No part of this publication nor any of the information herein may be quoted from, nor reproduced, in any form, including but not limited to: printing, scanning, photocopying, or any other printed, digital, or audio formats, without prior express written consent of the copyright holder.

**This book is a work of fiction. Any similarities to persons, living or dead, places of business, or situations past or present, is completely unintentional.

CHAPTER ONE

Every business owner dreams of success. Visions of crowds of eager customers and business hours so busy the line still stretched out the door at closing time were happy fantasies. Lydia Thackery had come to the realization that she had not been ready for that fantasy to become a reality. She was glad that the steakhouse she owned with her ex-husband was doing well, she really was. She just wished she had been more prepared for some of the consequences of that.

"I thought we agreed to do a parsley sprig as garnish on our whipped potatoes," Jeremy said, pausing as he hurried past Lydia with a bowl of veggies in his hands.

Jeremy was her ex-husband. They got along well, as long as they only communicated via text or email and never had to actually work together or see each other. She still wasn't sure whether it was a blessing or a curse that weekends had gotten busy enough that they were starting to need two chefs on shift just to keep the kitchen from getting bogged down. She had worked with Hank, their semiretired part-time chef last weekend. That had been fine. This weekend, however, she was working alongside Jeremy for the first time since their divorce over five years ago.

It wasn't going well. The only silver lining was that the shift was almost over. The kitchen stopped taking orders at ten, and the clock on the wall told her it was nine fifty-nine. They needed to deep clean the kitchen for the week ahead once they got all the orders in, but at least she wouldn't be working shoulder to shoulder with him the whole time.

"No, we decided to go with the butter boat instead, unless they ask for gravy. *Then* we do the garnish," she said.

"Are you sure? I don't remember talking about that."

"We discussed it two weeks ago, and you were texting Melanie during the whole meeting, so I'm not surprised you don't remember any of it," she snapped. Then she paused to take a deep breath. "Sorry. It's been a long day. We need to stop nitpicking at each other if we're going to keep doing this."

She was guilty of it too. While their divorce had been amicable, it hadn't been pleasant, and she thought they both would have been happier if they could have made a clean break. Neither of them had been willing to give up the restaurant, which meant they were in this for life.

"We need to be on the same page about things," he grunted before continuing past her. She sighed. It didn't sound like he was agreeing with her so much as accusing her. She thought they *had* been on the same page, but apparently him nodding and saying, "Uh-huh, sure," didn't count.

She was glad he and Melanie were dating again and taking things seriously this time, she really was, but would it kill him to be professional while he was working?

"Oh! I can sauté the veggies mix," a feminine voice said, making Lydia look up again in time to see Mira, their junior chef, take the bowl of chopped vegetables away from Jeremy. "You're busy, let me deal with this."

Lydia's eyes narrowed. Over the past couple of weeks, she had picked up on a concerning trend. It had been hard to notice at first, because she didn't usually have much to do with the schedule unless she needed to mark a specific day off, but she had noticed that Mira had started to almost exclusively work the same shifts Jeremy did. And all day today, the first time she and Jeremy had shared a shift, Mira had been focused almost entirely on him, to the point that she was only a step below blatantly flirting with him.

Jeremy seemed oblivious, and she knew him well enough to know he would never consider dating one of their employees, even if she wasn't a decade younger than him and he wasn't already in a committed relationship with someone else. She didn't have to *like* him to *trust* him. And she could hardly fault Mira if she was developing feelings for him, since she knew it wasn't something anyone could control, but the whole thing still seemed to spell disaster. The last thing they needed right now was one of their most-needed employees leaving because she had an unrequited crush on her boss.

She wanted to nip it in the bud but didn't know how. Regardless, it was a concern for another day. She couldn't spare the emotional energy to worry about it right now.

The door to the kitchen swung open and Penny, one of their newer servers, came in and promptly made her way to the small table in their break corner. Lydia finished plating what should be their second to last order for the night, glanced into the pan where Jeremy was sautéing the veggies to make sure he was on track to finish the last order, then made her way over to Penny, who had her head down on the table.

"I know it's been a long shift, but we'll get through it," she said, hoping to cheer the younger woman up. "We'll have more people working next weekend, so it shouldn't be as bad."

"It's not that," Penny mumbled. Something about her tone made Lydia realize that the younger woman wasn't just exhausted. Something was wrong.

Before she could ask, Gābe, another one of their servers, came in and made a beeline over to the table when he saw Penny. "Are you all right? You seemed pretty upset out there."

Penny mumbled something unintelligible at the table. Lydia frowned, glancing between her and Gabe. "What happened out there?"

With a sigh, Penny sat up straight and said, "My old boss is out there. I had to take his order. I didn't even realize it was him until I was already at the table, so I wasn't prepared at all. I hate him so much." She sniffed, and Lydia realized she was on the verge of tears. "I left my old job because of him, but I didn't expect him to still be able to make me feel this terrible."

"I don't need the details," Lydia said gently. "You don't have to go back out there if he makes you uncomfortable."

"Yeah, I'll take care of it," Gabe said, his jaw clenched. He looked like he disliked this guest he had never met as much as Lydia did. She considered asking Penny's old boss to leave without serving him but realized that might make more trouble for Penny than if she just avoided him.

"Thanks," Penny muttered. "He ordered the shrimp risotto, extra shrimp." She sniffed again, but seemed to be feeling a little better now that she knew she wouldn't need to go back out there. "I'd give him extra napkins too. The man eats like a pig."

Normally, Lydia wouldn't tolerate her employees making fun of the guests, even in the privacy of the kitchen, but it was clear Penny had some serious personal issues with this man, so she let it go.

"I'll get started on the order, and we'll send Gabe out with it," she said. "It should be the last order, so you can just stay in here and help with cleanup until he leaves. Take a few minutes to yourself first, if you need them."

Penny gave her a weak but grateful smile, and Lydia left Gabe to keep her company while she got started on the order. The shrimp risotto had to be made from scratch, which meant it would take about twenty minutes to get out, but she decided to kill two birds with one stone and make enough for her own dinner. She hadn't eaten since breakfast and the risotto sounded good enough to her, though right now she would eat just about anything. Plus, since she was making it at the same time as their last order, she would have time to scarf some down before they started cleaning.

She started by setting a pot of chicken broth on a burner to get it up to a simmer and called out to ask Mira to chop some shallots and mince some garlic, then peel some shrimp for her. While she waited, she drizzled avocado oil in another stockpot and set the heat to medium, then measured out the dry rice she would need.

Jeremy, who had just finished his last order — a medium-rare sirloin that Lydia had to admit looked absolutely perfect — peered into the bowl she had measured the rice into.

"That seems like too much rice," he said.

"I'm making extra for myself," she replied, trying hard to keep the annoyance out of her voice. The fact that he thought she didn't know how much rice a dish *she had come up with* needed made her almost irrationally angry, but both of their tempers were frayed after the long shift, and an argument wouldn't help anything.

As she scraped the chopped shallots off the cutting board and into the pot to sauté them, she knew today had solidified one thing for her.

She never wanted to work side by side with her ex-husband again.

CHAPTER TWO

Risotto wasn't hard to make, but it required a lot of attention. It needed to be stirred constantly while she slowly mixed in the simmering chicken broth to cook the rice. Keeping the heat low was the key, since the rice would burn otherwise, but it also meant that the rice cooked slowly. She didn't need to be constantly focusing on it, but it was close and was one of their more time consuming dishes to make.

Lydia had to divide her attention between stirring the chicken broth and a cup of white wine into rice and cooking the shrimp in a pan with butter and garlic while the kitchen staff started cleaning up around her. They couldn't use any cleaning sprays while she was cooking, but simple vinegar, hot water, and a rag to wipe everything up could go a long way toward cleaning up. Jeremy seemed to have realized he was hungry too, because he was frying a burger for himself on the stove beside her.

She had just determined that the rice had reached the right level of tenderness and turned the heat down so she could add butter and freshly grated parmesan when a loud crash from behind her made her jump. She turned around, wooden spoon still in hand, to see that someone had knocked over a large stock pot that must have been full of water to soak some tough spots off the counter. There was dirty water everywhere, and the pot was still rolling across the floor, along with a few utensils and a broken plate that must have been soaking inside of it.

She winced and decided to go help clean it up. The risotto was almost done anyway, and everyone was at the ends of their ropes. She didn't want anyone taking their anger out on the poor dishwasher who had messed up.

Jeremy was still busy with his hamburger patty, so she asked the first other person she saw, who happened to be Penny. She and Gabe were standing nearby, waiting for her to finish the order so Gabe could take it out. She hated to ask since it wasn't Penny's job, but she only needed her help for a few seconds.

"Can you take over? Just stir it slowly. I'll send Mira over to finish it."

Penny took the spoon from her, and Lydia glanced around the kitchen for Mira, who was getting cleaning supplies out of the cupboard in preparation for their deep clean. "Mira, can you finish up the risotto? I need to help clean this up," she called out. "Wash up first."

Mira nodded and set the armful of cleaning supplies down on the counter before making her way over to the sink to scrub her hands. Satisfied that she would take care of the risotto, Lydia ducked into the storage room and grabbed an armful of clean towels to clean the water up with, and a broom to sweep up the broken pieces of the plate. The dishwasher who had been responsible for knocking the pot over helped, so it didn't take too long to get the mess cleaned up.

She stood up just in time to see Jeremy hang his apron up on a hook in the break corner. Mira had abandoned the risotto to pack his burger into a to-go box, and Penny was helping Noel refill drink orders for the few remaining guests in the dining area, which left poor Gabe to stir the risotto. He looked uncomfortable, like he had been roped into it.

Lydia felt a spark of anger toward Mira. Crush on Jeremy or not, the junior chef should *not* have abandoned a task Lydia had specifically asked her to do just to help Jeremy with something he probably hadn't even asked her to do. She didn't think he was lazy enough to call Mira away from a task just to box up a burger for him.

She quickly washed her hands then returned to the stove. "I'll take over, Gabe. Thanks."

"Good, because I have no idea what I'm doing," he said with a weak chuckle. "Mira just told me to stir it."

To be fair, that was all it really needed at the moment—the goal was to melt the butter and the parmesan flakes slowly, giving the risotto the creaminess it was known for—but still, she had specifically asked Mira to finish it. With a sigh, she spooned the butter garlic shrimp into the pot with the risotto and gently folded it into the rice. There. It was done.

As she reached for a plate, she noticed a can of oven cleaner sitting on the counter next to the stove and made a mental note to do a refresher of their policies at the next staff meeting. She didn't like having dangerous chemicals out while the kitchen was still active. Nothing toxic should ever be near the food. She knew no one was planning on using any of the cleaners Mira had gotten out until after they were done cooking, but she thought it would be best if they left everything in the cupboard until the kitchen was officially closed for the day.

She plated the risotto and set it on the counter before calling out to Gabe, who had moved away to chat to Penny and Noel. "Order's ready!"

He hurried back over to grab the plate and then left the kitchen. She felt a rush of relief as the door swung shut behind him. Their last order of the day was out. She might not be done working, but at least she had a few minutes to sit and eat before she helped with the cleaning.

"I'm heading out," Jeremy announced by the door to no one in particular, his to-go box in one hand. "I'll see everyone tomorrow."

A few people gave half-hearted goodbyes, and Lydia summoned just enough energy to raise a hand in a wave farewell. It rankled a little that he was leaving without helping them clean, but to be fair, he *had* overseen their last deep clean, and it really didn't need both of them here. Besides, she couldn't blame him for wanting to get out of here. Cleaning would probably be a lot less stressful now that they were out of each other's hair.

She spooned the rest of the risotto into a bowl and carried it over to the table in the break corner. She didn't feel bad about eating while her employees worked; they all got a mandated half-hour long break each shift. They had been busy enough today that even with Jeremy's help, they had both worked through the entire shift. Everyone else had at least *some* time to eat and rest during the day, and she needed a few minutes to herself to recharge enough to see the rest of the evening through.

After setting her bowl down, she got up to pour herself a glass of water, which she downed before refilling it and bringing it back over to the table. She really could use a cup of coffee, but it was nearly ten thirty in the evening. She knew no matter how much she wanted the energy right now, she was going to regret it when she got home and couldn't get to sleep.

Finally sitting down, she sighed and took a moment to close her eyes and just relax. They needed to hire more employees. There was no question in her mind about that anymore. No one could keep going like this without burning out eventually.

Summoning her reserves of energy, she opened her eyes and picked up her spoon. Scooping up a bite with both rice and shrimp, she blew on it for a second before raising it to her lips. She paused before the food touched her mouth.

Something was … off. She had made this risotto a hundred times, and she knew exactly what it was supposed to smell like. Rich, with scents of butter, parmesan cheese, garlic, and a hint of the white wine that had gone into it.

It smelled like all of that, but there was an additional smell that gave her pause. A strange, chemical scent that shouldn't have been possible, given that she knew every single ingredient she had put into the dish.

Slowly, she lowered the spoon, then raised the entire bowl up to sniff it. The smell was definitely coming from the risotto. She felt the hair on the back of her neck prickle.

Something was wrong with the food.

CHAPTER THREE

"Mira, hold on," she called out when she noticed the other woman was carrying the risotto pot over to the sink. The junior chef paused, giving her a confused look.

"What's up?"

"Something smells weird." She stood up. Mira was still giving her a weird look, but she handed the pot over when Lydia gestured for it, raising an eyebrow as Lydia sniffed it.

"I didn't smell anything," she said. "Do you think the shrimp's bad?"

"No…" Lydia frowned. "That's not it. Can you smell it and tell me what you think?"

Mira made a face but did as she requested, sniffing the inside of the stockpot she had cooked the risotto in. Her expression changed from skeptical to surprised, then confused.

"You're right, it does smell weird. Maybe the cream was off?"

"There's no cream in our risotto," Lydia replied. Mira flushed, and she felt bad about it, but at the same time, Mira should be familiar enough with their menu by now to know that. Some people *did* add cream to risotto, but Lydia preferred making it the traditional way, and she and Jeremy had agreed on this recipe a long time ago.

"I don't know what it could be, then," she muttered. "Sorry."

"It reminds me of some sort of cleaner," Lydia said, frowning down at the pot. She thought about the armful of cleaning chemicals Mira had taken out of the cupboard, and the oven cleaner that had been sitting right next to the stove when she finished the risotto and felt her stomach clench. There was no way … but she had to check.

Asking Mira not to touch the pot just yet, she set it down on the counter and hurried over to the other side of the kitchen. The oven cleaner was still in the same spot, so she grabbed it and carried it over to the sink.

"Stand back," she warned to the employees who were standing nearby. Once people were clear, she took the top off of the cleaner and sprayed a short burst of it into the empty side of the sink. Then, she did something that she knew was probably a terrible idea, but she had to *know*.

She leaned forward and sniffed it.

The scent was chemical enough to make her feel sick, and it confirmed what she had feared. It was the same smell as the one in the risotto. Somehow, oven cleaner had ended up in her risotto.

No. Not just her risotto. It had been in the pot too. Whatever happened had happened while it was still cooking, which meant that the contaminants would be in the risotto she had sent out for their guest as well.

"Oh, my goodness," she whispered before dropping the spray can of oven cleaner in the sink and rushing out of the kitchen. She had never met Penny's ex-boss face to face and already disliked him for engendering such a negative response in the young woman, but regardless of her feelings toward him, he didn't deserve to be *poisoned.*

She skidded to a halt just inside the dining area as she realized she had no idea what the man she was looking for looked like or even where he was seated. She spotted Gabe sweeping up with the other servers and hurried over to him.

"Gabe, who's the man who ordered the risotto?" she asked.

He opened his mouth to respond but faltered when he saw her face. She had no idea what her expression looked like, but she knew it must be bad.

"Is everything all right?"

"Where is he?" she asked. "This is an emergency, Gabe. I think the risotto is poisoned."

He went pale. "He's—he's in the restroom. I saw him get up a minute ago."

"Did he eat the risotto? What table was he at?"

"I don't know. Um, his table's over there." He pointed at a table against the wall. She glanced toward it.

Even from this distance, she could see that at least half of the risotto was gone.

"Call an ambulance!" she commanded before she turned away to rush toward the men's restroom.

She shoved the door open, and saw a rotund man hunched over a sink, alternatively drinking water and spitting it out. His face was pink and shiny with sweat, and he looked extremely uncomfortable.

He looked up at her as she gazed at him helplessly. Then someone tried to open the door to the restroom, and it bumped into her, so she stepped aside to let Gabe come in. Noel was close behind him, with her phone pressed to her ear. Her eyes widened when she saw the man and the blood in the sink.

"Lydia, they said an ambulance is on the way, but they need to know what was in the food."

"Oven cleaner," Lydia whispered.

Noel related that information, then asked, "What brand?"

Lydia shook her head. She didn't know. She heard Noel tell Gabe to go figure it out, and she took a step toward the man, who looked terrified.

"Sir, what's your name?" she asked gently.

"Josh," he said, his voice hoarse. "Josh Moore. What's wrong with me? Everything hurts. What did you do?"

"The paramedics want to talk to you," Noel said, pushing past Lydia as she set her phone to speaker, so they could all hear the dispatcher's questions and instructions for Josh while she waited to hear back from poison control.

Lydia took a step back, knowing there wasn't anything she could do. She felt sick to her stomach even though she hadn't eaten a single bite of the risotto, and she knew it was because as much as she wanted to deny it, her gut was certain of the truth.

That oven cleaner hadn't gotten into the risotto on accident. Someone had poisoned the food on purpose. What she *didn't* know was why. Did someone want to kill Josh? Her? Were they just hoping to cause as much chaos and tragedy as possible?

While the motive for poisoning the food might be blurry, there was one more thing she was certain about. Whoever slipped the oven cleaner into the risotto had to have been in the kitchen while she was making it, which meant the poisoner was either one of her employees … or Jeremy himself.

She didn't think her ex-husband would poison her. She didn't *want* to think it. She and Jeremy didn't like each other very much, but they didn't hate each other either. They were committed to working together for the good of the restaurant, and even though they weren't perfect, they had both put more effort into their working relationship than they had into their marriage.

Or so she thought. Jeremy had been *right next to her* while she was cooking the risotto, and he had left the restaurant as soon as possible. He had known half the food was for her, and today had been an especially bad day as far as working with each other went.

The thought of him *poisoning* not just her but an innocent man he had never even met seemed absurd, but so was the thought of one of her employees doing it. She trusted all of these people. She *liked* them. She couldn't believe any of them were killers.

But the evidence was killing a man right in front of her.

It seemed like hours until the paramedics arrived, but Lydia knew it was really only minutes. Someone had alerted her other employees to what was going on, and they were working together to keep the last few, curious guests away from the bathroom to give Josh space. As soon as the ambulance pulled up out front, everyone cleared out of the way. A police cruiser had followed it into the parking lot, and an officer escorted the paramedics in.

Lydia watched as the paramedics wasted no time in ushering Josh out of the restaurant. She didn't know what was in oven cleaner, but it was corrosive enough to clean the rock-hard, baked-on messes in their ovens, so she knew his prognosis couldn't be good. Time was of the essence, if he could even be saved.

Everyone, her employees and guests alike, watched as the ambulance pulled out of Iron and Flame's parking lot, its lights flashing and its siren howling. There was a hush, but it only lasted until the ambulance was out of sight down the road, then everyone started talking all at once.

Lydia realized she had to pull herself together. She took a deep breath and tried to think clearly, but it was hard. She could barely process what had just happened.

How close she had come to being poisoned too.

The officer was already questioning people, trying to figure out what had happened. As soon as he learned about the oven cleaner in the risotto, she knew everything was going to change. The only person she was *sure* didn't do it was herself.

But this officer wouldn't know that, and she was the chef who had completed the order. She was the obvious suspect.

CHAPTER FOUR

Thankfully, no one tried to arrest her that night. After extensive questioning, the officer sent everyone home, but warned them that they would need to be available for more questioning. As she started her vehicle, she watched him put crime scene tape across the restaurant's door. They wouldn't be able to reopen until a forensics team had a chance to go over everything inside and test the risotto to confirm what had happened. It was a waiting game for *everybody* right now. What happened next would depend on whether Josh lived or died.

It was well past midnight when she got home. She rarely stayed up this late, but even though she was exhausted down to her very bones, she didn't think she would be able to sleep if she went to bed. Instead, she made herself a cup of chamomile tea and sat down on the couch with her laptop. It might be better not to know, but she had to look it up.

What would happen if someone ingested oven cleaner?

As careful as she was with the ingredients in her food, she had never looked at the ingredients in her cleaners. They were already careful to avoid cross contamination and to follow the instructions on the bottle. She had barely thought about it at all, if she was being honest. All she cared about was that the cleaners did their jobs, so it was one less thing she had to worry about.

Looking into oven cleaner was an eye opener. The main ingredient was sodium hydroxide, which sounded familiar, but she had to look it up to be certain. Lye. The same thing used in making soap, though with more research, she learned it had other, less glamorous uses too.

And what she learned about ingesting it wasn't good, not that she had expected it to be. It was extremely caustic—it was the same stuff they used in drain cleaner, and was used to dissolve *bodies*, for goodness sakes—and it heated up upon contact with water, hot enough to cause burns. She realized that Josh drinking water and using it to rinse his mouth might have made things worse.

She definitely shouldn't have looked it up. Closing her laptop, she sipped her now cold tea, trying to calm the twisting feeling in her stomach. She wanted to call Jude, either to ask him to come over and keep her company or just to pour her heart out to him, but it was the early hours of the morning, and she knew he would be deep asleep.

Her life had been so full this past year that her house, despite the only other living thing in it being a houseplant, rarely felt too empty, but right now she wished she had a dog or even a cat to keep her company. Instead, she turned her TV on and flipped through the channels until she found a nature documentary. Leaving the volume low enough that it was just background noise, she sat there and stared at the screen, not really paying attention.

What happened today felt like the worst nightmare she could imagine.

She must have dozed off at some point, because when she woke up, pale morning light was streaming through the sheer curtains in her living room, the TV was playing a documentary about garbage collection, and she had a kink in her neck from falling asleep sitting up on the couch.

And her phone was ringing.

After a dazed second in which her foggy mind caught up with everything that happened the night before, she scrambled to grab her phone off of the coffee table before the call went to voicemail, knocking over the mug with the last of her tea in it in the process. The sight of Penny's name on the screen gave her pause, but only for a moment. Answering it, she pressed the button to put the call on speaker and said, "Hello?"

There hadn't been much tea in the cup, but she used a tissue from the box on the coffee table to start dabbing it up as Penny answered.

"Hey, Lydia." Penny and the other new employees had finally all gotten used to using her and Jeremy's first names. "Sorry if I woke you up. I thought you'd want to know… I mean, I'm sure it will be on the news, but I don't know if the police would think to tell you first…"

"Penny, what happened?" she asked, pausing in her efforts to clean up the spilled tea.

The younger woman took a deep breath. "Mr. Moore died in the hospital."

It took Lydia a moment to equate Mr. Moore with Josh, since she had been thinking of him by his first name. The instant she made the connection, she dropped the tissue she was using to clean the tea and stared at her phone.

"Are you still there?"

"Yeah," Lydia said. "Sorry, I'm just… Thank you for telling me."

"What's going to happen now?" Penny's voice sounded uncertain, scared.

"I don't know. No work for the time being, of course. Beyond that… I just don't know."

There wasn't much else to say after that. Lydia thanked Penny again for telling her and they exchanged brief goodbyes before they ended the call. Belatedly, she wondered if she should have asked if Penny was all right—of course she wasn't—and seen if there was anything she could do to help, but she felt like doubt and uncertainty had poisoned her.

Penny had hated Josh Moore, and Penny was one of the people who had access to the risotto. Lydia didn't want to think that the kind, quiet girl she had grown to know over the past few months would *kill* someone, but there was no denying that someone in that kitchen had done it, and Penny was the only one with motive.

Unless Lydia had been the target instead.

She checked the time on her phone. It was almost six in the morning. Jude would be up around seven-thirty. She could wait an hour and a half to call him. While she waited, she had to think about what to say … and what she was going to do.

After a shower, a change of clothes, and a cup of coffee, Lydia felt better, if only marginally. She sat at the kitchen table, where she could see the birds squabbling with the squirrels at the bird feeder her across-the-street neighbors had in their yard. It was such a cheerful sight, so at odds with what she was feeling.

It was finally late enough that Jude was probably up, so she got up to refill her coffee cup, then dialed his number. He answered after a few rings, and thankfully, it didn't sound like she had woken him up.

"Lydia? What's going on?"

He sounded pleased to hear from her but a little concerned, probably because she had never called him so early before. She had already gathered her thoughts enough that she knew what she wanted to say, so she launched right into it.

"Jude, something happened last night…" She told him about discovering that the risotto was poisoned, calling an ambulance for Josh, and then about Penny's bad news earlier this morning. Finally, she ended with a confession. "I don't know what to do or what's going to happen. I'm worried this might be the end of Iron and Flame."

It was the first time she had admitted that, even to herself. She felt horrible and selfish for worrying about the restaurant when a man was dead, but Iron and Flame had been the single most important thing in her life for years. It was her passion, her life's work. And she might lose it all.

"That's too much for anyone to deal with on their own," he said. "Do you want me to come over?"

"You'd have to call off of work," she said. He would do it, she knew, but it would just be one more thing she would feel bad about. "I think I'm going to need to talk to the police more, and I should get in touch with Jeremy and my employees as well. Plus, I need to come up with a statement to put on the restaurant's social media page…"

She trailed off. There was a lot she had to do.

"How about this evening?" he said. "I'll grab food for us, and Saffron and I will come over and keep you company until you kick us out."

She almost smiled, despite everything. "That sounds good. Thank you, Jude."

"Be safe," he said. "And if you need someone, even just for emotional support, call me. I'll be there if you need me."

She knew he would be. Knowing someone was in her corner gave her strength she hadn't realized she needed. Whatever happened after all of this, she genuinely had no doubt in her mind that Jude would be there for her. They might have only been dating for a few months, but they had known each other for well over a year, and at some point, she had fallen in love with him without even realizing it.

That was a revelation for another day, though. Right now, she needed to figure out who had poisoned the risotto and why. If Josh hadn't been their target, her own life might still be in danger.

CHAPTER FIVE

She called Jeremy next and wasn't surprised to find that he was already up too, if he had even gone to sleep at all. They needed to talk, but even though a large part of her refused to believe he would try to poison her, she was just wary enough not to want to meet him in private. She suggested Morning Dove, her favorite cafe, in half an hour, and he agreed.

She arrived first and got a table as far away from the window as she could. She didn't know how much of what happened at Iron and Flame was public knowledge, but she didn't want to attract too much attention if she could help it.

Cynthia, the woman who owned Morning Dove, brought her a carafe of coffee, which Lydia accepted even though she'd already had two cups, though she did ask for some water as well.

"I don't mean to pry," Cynthia said before leaving to get her water. "But is everything all right? I saw the crime scene tape on your restaurant's entrance when I came in to work this morning."

"I'm not sure how much I should say, but we'll be closed until further notice," Lydia said. "I can tell you more once I know how much the police are making public."

The other woman grimaced in sympathy. "Well, I hope whatever's going on isn't too bad. Let me know if there's anything I can do."

Lydia realized that Cynthia probably understood what she was going through better than almost anyone, since she had been in a similar position herself not too long ago. Lydia had helped Morning Dove recover some of its reputation after a customer passed away in the cafe, and she knew Cynthia was being genuine in her offer of giving similar help.

"Thanks," she said, offering the other woman a weak smile. "That means a lot to me."

Jeremy arrived a few minutes later and sat across from her at the table. He looked terrible, but she knew the only reason she didn't look equally as bad was because she had used makeup to disguise the circles under her eyes. She would be surprised if either of them got good sleep for a long time.

"What exactly happened? Have you heard anything new?" he asked as soon as he was seated. The police had told her they had already contacted him last night, but she hadn't been sure how much they told him. Apparently, it wasn't much.

"The victim passed away in the hospital last night," she said. He bowed his head, closing his eyes. One of his hands clenched slowly into a fist. When he didn't say anything, she carried on and briefly shared what happened from her perspective. "We need to figure out how to handle this."

"I don't know, Lydia. I'm not exactly thinking about our social media presence or whatever the locals are going to say about us right now."

"That's part of it, but that's not what I mean." She hesitated, glanced around to make sure Cynthia wasn't on her way back to take their order, then said,

"Someone poisoned that risotto, Jeremy. Someone who was in our kitchen while I was making it. It *has* to be one of our employees. There's no other option."

Well, there was, and she was looking him in the eye at this very moment, but no good could come from sharing those doubts with him. Either he would be—rightfully—offended that she would even consider him as a suspect, or in the off chance that he really had done something to the risotto, he might be in even more of a hurry to finish the job.

He buried his face in his hands with a quiet groan. When he looked up again, he said, "I didn't even consider that. No, there has to be something we aren't thinking of. Maybe someone snuck into the kitchen, or it was an accident…"

He trailed off, and she suspected that he realized how unlikely his words were. "We both know that's not possible. There was oven cleaner in a dish I had just made from scratch. It wasn't an accident. No one who didn't belong there could have been in the kitchen without one of us noticing. One of the people *we* hired did this."

"How can we reopen?" he asked in horror. "We can't risk it happening again."

"I agree," she said. She took in a deep breath and let it out slowly. This was what she needed to talk to him about more than anything. "I don't think we should reopen the restaurant after the police give us the all clear. Not until we know who did this. Not even if it takes months."

She held his gaze, expecting him to argue or ask how they were going to come back from an extended closure like that, but to her surprise, he looked almost ... relieved. "I agree," he said. "It's not worth the risk. The only other option is firing everyone who was there and rehiring a completely new team."

It *was* an option, but the thought left a bitter taste in her mouth. It would be horribly unfair to everyone other than the person who poisoned the risotto, and that person would still be out there in secret somewhere. Maybe if it really did take months, the majority of the employees would leave to find other jobs, but they would still have to rehire almost half their workforce, which wouldn't be easy.

She knew, and she knew Jeremy knew it too, that if they kept the restaurant closed for too long, there was a very good chance it might not reopen.

"Will you handle telling everyone, or should I do it?" he asked at last.

"I'll draft up an email to send to the team, if you come up with something to put on our social media page. I know it doesn't seem like the time to worry about that, but we *need* to say *something*, even if it's just to give condolences to his family. Email me the draft before you post it, and I'll do the same with the email before I send it to everyone else."

He nodded. There wasn't much to say after that. He left a few minutes later without having done more than drink half his coffee. Lydia ordered some hash browns, bacon, and scrambled eggs to go because she felt bad about leaving without ordering food, even though she felt too sick to her stomach from everything that happened to be very hungry. She still needed to eat, and at least this way, she wouldn't have to make anything.

She waited around long enough to get her to-go order, then thanked Cynthia, left her a sizable tip, and left the cafe, planning on heading back home to work on the email she needed to write to let her employees know what was going on.

Her mind was already working out what she was going to say, so she was only half paying attention as she stepped outside and held the door open for a couple who was on their way in. It was only when someone said, "Lydia?" that she blinked and realized the couple wasn't a couple at all—it was Penny and Gabe.

"Sorry, my head was in the clouds," she said. She let the door close since it was clear the two wanted to talk to her—they were hanging back on the sidewalk, standing side by side as they stared at her. Holding hands. Oh, they were a couple after all.

"Um, we were just getting breakfast," Penny said hesitantly.

"How are the two of you holding up?" she asked.

"I think we're both still in shock," Gabe said. "Well, I know I am, anyway. I'm guessing there's no work today?"

Lydia shook her head. "No. The restaurant is going to be closed indefinitely, though I'd appreciate it if you let me get the word out to everyone else before you tell them. I'm hoping to get the email sent this morning."

Gabe blanched, but Penny looked unsurprised. She squeezed his hand, then gave Lydia an embarrassed glance. "Thanks for telling us. Um, there's no policy against employees dating, is there? We weren't sure if we should tell you, or just be discreet while we're at work."

"No, there's no policy against it, and you didn't need to tell anyone," Lydia assured them. "All I'd ask is that you don't let your relationship affect your work, which you already have been doing just fine at. There's nothing to worry about."

"Oh, good," Penny said, looking relieved.

Lydia was beginning to feel a little awkward, and it was clear both of them did as well. They were out on a breakfast date, and chatting with their boss was probably the last thing they wanted to do. Thankfully, her cell phone rang, giving her an easy exit from the conversation. She said goodbye to them and waited until they were inside the cafe before she checked her phone, unable to forget her suspicions about Penny. Gabe had to be included in that, both because he had been in the kitchen when the risotto was poisoned, and now because she knew he was dating Penny, which meant he might have a motive to hurt someone who had hurt her.

Detective Bronner was calling. She had been expecting a call from the police anyway and was just glad it was from someone she sort of knew. She answered the call as she walked back to her SUV.

"This is Lydia speaking. How can I help you?"

"I'm sure you know what this call is about, Ms. Thackery," he said. "Can you meet me at your restaurant this morning?"

That was unexpected. She had assumed they would speak at the police station. "When? I'm at the cafe, so I could head over there right now." She could see her restaurant from here; it was kitty-corner across the block from Morning Dove.

"You do that, and I'll meet you there. Please don't enter the building without me."

She promised she wouldn't and ended the call as she got into her vehicle. Hopefully, the to-go breakfast she had with her would still be good to eat when she was done talking to the detective. She had no idea what to expect and was more than a little nervous as she pulled her vehicle onto the road to drive the short distance to Iron and Flame.

CHAPTER SIX

She only had to wait a few minutes for Detective Bronner to pull into the parking lot. As she got out of her SUV, she wondered what he was thinking. Did he consider her a suspect? As much as she hated the thought, she knew the answer was probably yes. She had made the risotto. And even if she hadn't added the poison directly, it had happened while she was working there, so it was her responsibility, at least a little.

Swallowing back against a feeling of guilt, she greeted the detective and followed him up to the restaurant's entrance. He removed the crime scene tape so they could go in, though she was sure he would replace it when they left.

Nothing had been cleaned up from the night before, but it was evident that at some point, probably recently, forensics had come and gone. It was strange, both to see the restaurant so messy and to know people had been in here without her or Jeremy there to keep an eye on things.

"Before we start, I'd like to ask if there's anything you want to tell me," Detective Bronner said.

She blinked, her mind blanking even though she was sure there probably *were* things she should tell him. Was he expecting a confession? Why did she feel so guilty all of a sudden, even though she was innocent?

"We've decided to keep the restaurant closed until the culprit is found," she said, latching onto the one somewhat relevant fact she could share with him. "Even if it takes months. Past that… Well, we'll see."

"Good, that's one of the things I was going to talk to you about," he said. "You should be clear to return here and clean everything up in a day or two, and I can't force you to stay shut any longer than that, but I strongly believe that reopening so soon could expose more people to the killer."

"Yeah, we came to the same conclusion." She sighed. "It has to be someone who was working last night. The killer is one of my employees."

Thankfully, he didn't say anything about *her* being a potential suspect, but she was certain he knew that she was smart enough to figure out she was on his radar. Instead, he asked, "What about Mr. Montrose?"

"It doesn't seem like something he would do." That was the truth, no matter her private doubts about him. Jeremy had never been violent or vengeful. He wasn't a perfect person, but he wasn't a cruel one either.

"Does it seem like something anyone you work with would do?"

She grimaced. "No. I know you're right, and I can't assume anyone's innocent. It's just hard. I've worked with some of them for years, you know?"

His expression softened, just slightly. "I understand that this is difficult. I'm sure you're wondering why I asked you to meet me here." He paused long enough for her to nod, then continued, "I'd like you to walk me through everything that happened last night. Be as specific as you can. Show me where each person was standing, show me where you normally keep your cleaning supplies, show me what burner you were using to cook. Every single detail you can remember. Try not to touch too much, but don't worry about it if you have to open doors or move something."

What he was asking was going to be difficult, because yesterday had been chaotic and she had been about at the end of her rope by the time she made the risotto, but she would try her best. Maybe walking through it would help her, too. Maybe she would remember something that would tell her which of her employees had done such a horrible thing.

It took them a surprisingly long time to go through it all, well over an hour. He would occasionally ask her to repeat something she had said minutes ago, and she wondered if he was prodding for holes in her story. She didn't care as much as she thought she would have. No, she hadn't poisoned Josh, but he was dead because of her—her restaurant, someone she hired, the risotto she had made. She wanted Detective Bronner to believe that she hadn't done it so he would have more time to focus his efforts on other people, but that was it.

Finally, she finished, and he didn't have any more questions about where everyone was standing and what they were doing the night before. He flipped through his notes for a few seconds before speaking.

"So, and please correct me if I'm wrong, only yourself, the two servers, Penny and Gabe, and the assistant chef, Mira, had direct contact with the risotto while it was cooking?"

"Mira's a junior chef, but yes," she said. "Jeremy was cooking on a burner next to me, but as far as I know, he didn't work on the risotto at all."

"How certain are you that none of your other employees was within arm's reach of the dish?"

She frowned, thinking back. Some of the other servers had come in and out, and their dishwasher had been working hard on the other side of the room. Noel had come in to refill drinks. Had any of them come near the stove? She didn't think so. Noel had been the closest, but she was busy, and the front-of-house staff tried to keep out of the way of the kitchen staff.

"Maybe eighty-percent sure," she said at last. "I don't *think* anyone other than myself, Jeremy, Penny, Gabe, and Mira were within arm's reach of the risotto, but I wasn't paying attention to where everyone was standing at the time. It was the end of an extremely long and stressful day, and I was just ready to be done."

"Can you tell me what in particular made yesterday so difficult?"

"Mostly it was that I was working with Jeremy," she admitted. Their difficulties in getting along felt like a personal failing to her, but now wasn't the time to keep quiet just because she was embarrassed. "We get along well enough to run the restaurant together, but not to work side by side, if that makes sense."

He nodded and made another note. "Ms. Thackery, can you think of anyone who might have a reason to try to kill you?"

"No," she said. "Not realistically, anyway. Jeremy and I have our issues, but I genuinely don't believe he wants me dead. I get along well with all of the staff, at least as far as I know." Even Mira; for all that she had a blatant crush on Jeremy, it wasn't as if she had anything against Lydia. It would have been clear to any of her employees that she and Jeremy had zero plans to ever get back together. "Do you think whoever poisoned the food was trying to kill me?"

"I'm covering all of my bases," he told her. "I suggest being careful, just in case. I will be looking into Mr. Moore as well. I believe I read in the case notes that one of your employees used to work for him?"

"Penny did," Lydia said. "I know she didn't like him. I'm not sure what the issue was, but it was bad enough that she was uncomfortable serving him, so Gabe, our other server, took his table instead."

He nodded and made a note, then closed his notepad with a snap. "I think that's all for right now. It's possible that we will need to ask you more questions in the future. Any plans to take a vacation anytime soon?"

"No. I don't plan on going further than Wausau to visit my sister for the foreseeable future."

"Please let me know if that changes. And please, if you learn anything about what happened, contact me immediately. It's possible your employees will share more with you than they are comfortable telling me, especially if they realize the restaurant won't reopen until this is solved. The threat of losing a job is enough to make a lot of people talk."

"Do you think someone saw something?" she asked.

He shrugged. "In a busy place like this kitchen, it's almost guaranteed that someone saw something, even if they don't realize it yet."

She agreed to tell him if any of her employees let anything slip or she learned anything more, and he escorted her out of the building. It felt strange to walk away from Iron and Flame knowing it might be months before it reopened, if it reopened at all.

CHAPTER SEVEN

Her reheated breakfast from the cafe was one of the more disappointing things she had eaten recently, through no fault of Cynthia's. Scrambled eggs just didn't reheat well. It didn't matter, anyway; she was eating because she needed to fuel her body, not out of any sort of enjoyment. She normally loved food—she believed eating should be an experience—but after everything that happened, she couldn't bring herself to focus on taste right now.

She had gone home after her meeting with Detective Bronner because there simply wasn't anything else she could do. She was supposed to be writing an email to let the staff know what was going on, but she had been staring at her open laptop without inspiration for the last twenty minutes. The blinking cursor and the blank page seemed to be taunting her.

This was possibly the most important staff email she had ever sent, and she had no idea how to start it. Or how to end it. Or anything in the middle. How could she tell her employees that they might be out of a job for months, or longer? They relied on the income from this job. One or two might still live with their parents, but most of them were self-sufficient. This email was going to affect all of them in a major way.

Somehow, she still hadn't completed it by the time Jude came over that evening. She had started and deleted parts of the email what felt like a hundred times, but nothing felt right. When Jude texted her that he was on his way with Chinese food, she decided to put a pin in it. She would finish it tomorrow, no matter what.

After possibly the most stressful day off in her entire life, seeing Jude and Saffron at her door was a relief. She took the bags of Chinese takeout from Jude and welcomed them in. Saffron, Jude's yellow mixed breed dog, greeted her with innocent joy, then pawed pointedly at her empty water dish, which Lydia refilled for her as soon as she set the bags down. Since her and Jude's work schedules never quite lined up, he often dropped Saffron off at her house so the dog would have more company during the day. Lydia had slowly accumulated enough pet supplies she probably wouldn't need to buy anything but food if she decided to get a dog of her own.

"Sorry we're a little later than I expected. How are you doing?" Jude asked.

"It's been kind of a terrible day, if I'm being honest," she said. "I don't know what's going to happen to the restaurant or the employees, and on top of all of that, I've been feeling guilty about what happened to Josh, the man who died."

He pulled her into a hug, which made her feel better even though she knew there wasn't much Jude could actually *do*. He was a game warden, and since Josh's death hadn't involved wild animals or the state forest, it wasn't exactly in his jurisdiction.

"Do you want to talk about it or not talk about it?"

"I don't think I'll be able to focus on anything if we don't talk about it," she said. "Let's sit down with the food first, though. I haven't eaten anything since breakfast. I didn't even realize how hungry I was until I smelled that Chinese food."

"I figured we could use some comfort food tonight," he said, moving over to the cupboard to take some plates out. "You sit down and relax. I'll set the table and bring everything over."

It was amazing how much better everything felt with some company and a good meal in front of her. She took a few minutes to think while they started eating, and finally realized what part of the problem she was having with the email was.

"I think Jeremy and I need to meet with the staff in person," she said. She explained about the email she was supposed to send out, and her and Jeremy's decision to close the restaurant indefinitely. "It's just too much, too *big*, to tell them in an email. We need to have a staff meeting. I'm just not sure where."

"Ah, I suppose the restaurant isn't an option," he said, considering the problem. "Would it be inappropriate to have it at your house?"

"In normal circumstances, I would be fine with it, but it feels risky," she said. "Whoever poisoned that risotto was working at the restaurant last night, and, well, there's no guarantee I wasn't the target. I'd be inviting the killer into my home."

He grimaced. "Right. I hadn't thought of how small the suspect pool is, or that the suspect is almost definitely someone you know. Are you sure having a staff meeting at all is a good idea?"

"It has to be done, I think. If we do it somewhere public, and everyone's there, it should be safe enough." She paused. "I don't think we should have food though."

"If you're looking for somewhere public, how about that little park in town? They have those pavilions with picnic tables, and I think the weather is supposed to be decent this week."

"That's a good idea." She would have to talk to Jeremy about it and figure out *when* to meet, but at least she had a plan. This felt *right*, a lot better than sending an email to explain everything.

"Do you have any gut feelings about who's responsible?" he asked.

"Honestly? No. One of my employees, Penny, used to work for the man who died, and I know they had some sort of bad history between them. She didn't even want to leave the kitchen while he was there. She might have a motive. And this morning, I just found out Gabe, one of our other new servers, is dating her, so I suppose he might too, but it's hard to believe it. These are people I've worked beside almost daily for months."

"You said you're not certain that *you* weren't the target," he said. "Why?"

"Well, the dish that was poisoned was our last order of the day, a risotto I made a double order of. Josh had ordered it, and I decided to make extra for myself so I wouldn't have to take the time to cook something else. I told Jeremy what I was doing because he commented on the amount of rice I was using, but I'm sure he wasn't the only one who heard. Whoever poisoned it knew I was going to eat it. I don't think any of them would want to poison me—if I did, they wouldn't be working there—but it wouldn't be smart to pretend it wasn't a possibility."

"None of them have anything to gain by you being out of the picture?" he asked.

She frowned. She hadn't thought of it quite like that before. Jeremy immediately came to mind. They had both agreed that their half of the restaurant should go to the other person if one of them passed away unexpectedly, with a clause that they could come to a new agreement if one of them had children. Was getting the restaurant to himself enough of a motive for him to want her dead? They'd had more disagreements about how to run the restaurant than usual this past year, but the thought of him jumping straight to something as extreme as *murder* seemed insane.

Mira was the only other person she could think of who might have a motive, though hers was even flimsier than Jeremy's. All Lydia had to go on was a sneaking suspicion the younger woman had a crush on Jeremy. If she went so far as to schedule her shifts only on the days he worked, maybe trying to get the ex-wife out of the way wasn't completely out of the question.

She shared her thoughts with Jude, then let out a deep sigh. "Despite all of that, and knowing that they're the *only options,* it's still almost impossible for me to believe it. This whole thing has been a nightmare, and I don't know when it's going to end. It's terrifying, not knowing what the restaurant's future holds. Even if the killer was arrested tomorrow, could we survive the damage to our reputation?"

"I think you'll be able to pull the restaurant through," he said. "No matter what happens, I'll be here for you, and I'll help you however I can. There will be a light at the end of the tunnel eventually."

She knew he was right, but it was scant hope when she had no idea how far away that light would be.

CHAPTER EIGHT

In the morning, she got Jeremy on board with the staff meeting and sent her employees a much more simple email asking them to meet her at the small park in the center of Quarry Creek at eleven on Wednesday morning so they could discuss the events of the weekend and what they were going to do moving forward.

She also proofread the post Jeremy had come up with for their social media page. It was a simple yet heartfelt post giving their condolences to Josh's family and a notice that the restaurant would be closed until further notice.

It felt good to have at least the next few steps planned out and to have finished the email, but Lydia found herself at loose ends for the rest of the day. It seemed wrong to try to relax, but until the police contacted her, there wasn't much she could do. Maybe someone would let something slip at the staff meeting, but that was still two days away.

Jude had dropped Saffron off that morning, so at least she had some company. She took the dog for a walk, told herself she was definitely going to start jogging again when all of this was over, then took her cell phone into her backyard to call her sisters while Saffron sniffed every blade of grass to make sure nothing interesting had happened back there since the day before.

Lillian used to live just a few minutes away in downtown Quarry Creek but had moved to Wausau a few weeks ago for a great new job. It was still a little strange knowing her sister wasn't in town anymore, but things hadn't changed much overall. They still got together a couple of times a month for breakfast. It was just a slightly longer drive.

Her half-sister, Marcy, lived even farther away, and Lydia had only seen her twice since she learned about her existence. Maybe if the restaurant closed permanently, she would have more time to travel.

Shaking her head and reminding herself that nothing was certain yet, she started a group call between her and her two sisters. They both worked office jobs with normal lunch hours, so she was hoping they would have the chance to talk. She needed to explain what was going on. While she wasn't looking forward to reliving the entire, horrible story, she knew in their position, she would want to be kept in the loop.

Thankfully, both of them were available for a quick chat, and Lydia recited a summarized version of the weekend. Lillian immediately offered to help her find a criminal defense lawyer if she needed one, and Marcy was aghast at the thought that she had almost died.

Talking to them was good. It was a reminder that life went on. She had to strong-arm them into changing the subject and talking about what was going on in their own lives but hearing that they were both doing well filled her with nothing but happiness.

"I have to get going in a minute," Marcy said towards the end of their conversation. "But before I do, I wanted to talk to the two of you about something. I'm thinking of moving a little closer to the two of you. Now that Landon's away at college, I'm starting to realize how lonely I am here. I don't have a husband or even any close friends outside of the office. I know we didn't grow up together, but I'd really like to be closer to the two of you. I don't want to be weird and clingy, though, so please tell me if you want me to stay far away."

"Are you kidding? We'd love to have you closer," Lydia said.

"Yeah, we'd both like to get to know you better too," Lillian said. "And we might not have known about you until earlier this year, but we're still family."

"Thank you both. You're so kind," Marcy said. "It will be a while before I make any big moves. I'll need to find another job and a place to live, and I'm not sure yet what the timeline will be. I'll keep you updated."

"I'll let you know if I hear of anything good in Wausau," Lillian said.

"And I'll do the same for Quarry Creek," Lydia promised.

She felt a pang at the thought that the restaurant might be closed for good by the time Marcy moved here but tried to ignore it. The restaurant closing permanently was the worst-case scenario, short of someone else being killed.

Her phone vibrated, and she pulled it away from her ear long enough to see that she had an email from Jeremy. "Hey, I've got to go. I'll let you both know if there are any big updates."

Marcy and Lillian both said goodbye, and she ended the call. Saffron trotted over to her and rested her head on Lillian's knee. Lillian scratched her ears with one hand while she opened the email with the other.

She hadn't been sure what to expect of the email. It had no subject line, but that was an annoying habit of Jeremy's, so it wasn't surprising. What was surprising was that he had forwarded her another email and added a note that read, *Why is Mira acting like I'm on death's door? I'm not the one who almost got poisoned.*

Frowning, Lydia read through Mira's email.

Jeremy,

I know this might be crossing boundaries, but I wanted to let you know I'm here for you if you need any support or just want to talk. I'm free all day today and tomorrow if you want to meet up before the staff meeting. I hope you're doing well, or as well as can be.

Love,

Mira

Jeremy was ... obtuse. Lydia felt some satisfaction in having solid evidence that her gut feeling about Mira was right, but the younger woman seemed to be aware that her actions were becoming inappropriate, and it wasn't stopping her.

It might be time to tell Jeremy directly in hopes that he would put a stop to it before things spiraled out of control. It was obvious he wasn't going to put two and two together himself.

She typed and sent a response.

I think we need to talk about something. Can we meet before Wednesday?

He didn't answer until she was back inside, sharing a snack of string cheese with Saffron. She tossed the rest to the dog, who caught it with a snap of her teeth, then read the email.

Melanie and I can come over this evening. What time works for you?

Melanie was coming along? She didn't mind, she and Melanie got along well despite how strange their relationship was. Most women Jeremy had dated weren't fans of him working with his ex-wife and were snide and rude to Lydia. Melanie had gone the opposite direction and made an effort to be her friend. Still, spending time with both of them was bound to be awkward.

On the other hand, having Melanie around might be a good thing. Her heart told her Jeremy wasn't the one who poisoned the risotto, but her heart also told her *none* of her staff had done it, so she knew for a fact her heart was wrong about at least one of them. Having Jeremy over wasn't the smartest move she could make right now, but she doubted he would try to finish her off with Melanie in the next room.

Anytime, just give me twenty minutes notice so I can tidy up.

She only realized after she sent the email that Melanie's presence might make the conversation about Mira even more uncomfortable than it would have been already, but it was too late to change her mind.

CHAPTER NINE

While she waited for Jeremy and Melanie to come over, Lydia tidied her house, even though it didn't really need it, and put some coffee on, which she definitely *did* need. She made sure Saffron had fresh water in her bowl, checked the pothos that hung over her sink to see if the soil in its pot was getting too dry, and double-checked her call log to make sure she hadn't missed anything from the police.

She knew it had only been two days, but she hoped they would make some progress soon.

Jeremy's car pulled into her driveway just after five. She grabbed a bag of dog treats and made Saffron wait a few feet back, tossing the dog a treat every few seconds to encourage her to stay. She managed to hold herself back even as Lydia opened the door and greeted Jeremy and Melanie.

"Come on in," she said, stepping back to let them through. "Feel free to make yourselves at home."

"Aww, who's this?" Melanie asked, making a beeline for Saffron, whose self-control finally broke. She rushed forward, her entire body wriggling with how hard her tail was wagging and greeted Melanie like an old friend.

"She's Jude's dog. Her name's Saffron. She's very friendly, but I can put her outside if she's too much of a distraction."

"No, she's fine," Melanie said. "I love dogs, but I'm allergic to them. It's not bad if I'm over at someone's house for a couple of hours, but any longer than that, and my nose won't stop running. Did he move in with you?"

"No, we're good company for each other while he's at work, so he drops her off here in the mornings sometimes. Can I get either of you anything to drink? I just made coffee, and I also have tea and orange juice, plus water of course."

"I wouldn't mind some coffee," Melanie said, straightening up. "Jeremy?"

Satisfied that Melanie was firmly in the category of friend, Saffron padded over to investigate Jeremy, who gave her a stiff pat on the head. He looked like he wasn't sure what the etiquette was for meeting his ex-wife's boyfriend's dog.

"I'm good, thanks," he said.

"Do you mind if I use your restroom, Lydia?" Melanie asked. "We have a lot to talk about, and I don't want to be distracted during the conversation."

"Of course, it's just down the hall. It's the door on your right, before the living room."

Lydia pointed the way, trying not to let her curiosity make her impatient. She had thought Mira was the only thing they needed to talk about, but from the sound of it, they had something they wanted to discuss with her, too. Melanie's presence was starting to make more sense, though she couldn't imagine what they wanted to talk to her about. Jeremy's relationships were none of her business, and vice versa.

"We shouldn't start until she gets back, but in your email, you said you wanted to talk?" Jeremy said. "What's that about?"

Right, this would actually be a little easier to handle while Melanie was indisposed.

"Why don't you sit down?" she suggested as she took a mug for Melanie out of the cupboard.

She didn't know how the other woman liked her coffee, so she set cream, milk, and sugar on the counter next to it, along with a spoon to stir it. Then, she joined Jeremy at the table, sitting across from him. Saffron came to lean against her legs, and Lydia stroked the dog's fur as she gathered her thoughts.

"Has she told you something? Is she planning on quitting?" he asked. "Or do you think she had something to do with the poisoned food?"

"None of that," Lydia said. "Well, maybe the last, but only because everyone who was there that night is a suspect. No, this is something a little more … delicate." She paused, but he looked clueless, so she decided to just spit it out. "She's clearly obsessed with you, and it's reaching a point where we need to decide how we're going to address it."

He looked floored. "Mira? Are you sure?"

She nodded. "I didn't put it together until we all worked together on Saturday. I knew she had been requesting all the same shifts as you, but it took me being there to see it. She's hyperaware of where you are whenever you're both in the kitchen. She'll drop everything to help you do things you don't even need help with, like boxing up that burger. She talks to you a lot differently than she talks to me or the other employees. And that email cinches it. She's on the verge of becoming a stalker, Jeremy."

"I had no clue," he said. "I thought she was just getting serious about learning the ropes in the kitchen. What should I do?"

"I don't know. Let's get past this staff meeting and figure out where the restaurant is headed. In the meantime, maybe you should forward any messages she sends you to me, and don't contact her directly." She smiled wryly. "It's almost a shame we're not big enough to need a human resources department, because this is the sort of thing they're perfect for."

"Do you think your sister would have any useful advice? If so, you'll have to be the one to talk to her. She still hates my guts."

"I'll give her a call sometime this week."

Jeremy swore suddenly, startling both her and Saffron, who barked. "I just thought of something. About two weeks ago, Melanie and I had dinner at Iron and Flame, and she had what she thinks is food poisoning later that night. We figured it was probably something she ate earlier, since we know the kitchen at the restaurant is clean and we aren't serving bad food, but what if Mira did something to it? I don't remember if she was working that night or not. It was on my day off, so I don't know what the schedule looked like."

Lydia's eyes widened. "This could be huge. Send me a text with the day and time you went in, and I'll see if I can find the schedule from that week. I usually take a picture of them with my phone so I can check it when I'm away from the restaurant, so I should still have it."

He gave her a tight nod. "Let me know what you find. If she's behind all of this, if she tried to poison Melanie, I'm going to make sure she regrets it if it's the last thing I do."

"Even if we figure out that she was working that evening, it doesn't prove anything," she reminded him. "We'll take the information to the police, and Melanie can make a statement, but that's it. We can't let this slip, Jeremy. If she *did* do it, and she somehow figures out that we know, I have no idea what she'll do. If she's obsessed with you enough to try to kill me and maybe even your girlfriend, then she's going to be completely unpredictable. Are you going to be able to act normally when you see her at the staff meeting on Wednesday?"

He grimaced. "I'll try. I don't know how well it will go, though. Even if we don't find any proof she's behind the poisoning, I'm not going to be able to pretend we didn't have this discussion. She might notice something's off."

Lydia sighed. "Well, you'll just have to do your best."

She heard the door to the bathroom open, and Melanie came back into the kitchen. She looked between the two of them and raised her eyebrows.

"Wow, there's a heavy mood in here. What did I miss?"

Lydia had no idea if she could trust Melanie to keep everything quiet until the police had worked it out, but since she had told Jude everything, it would have been hypocritical of her to ask Jeremy not to tell the person he was dating. She waited while Jeremy gave Melanie a condensed version of their conversation. Melanie listened as she fixed herself a cup of coffee, and looked shocked as she joined them at the table.

"That's a lot. Thank you for telling him about Mira, Lydia. We appreciate it."

"I figured he should know before things spiraled out of control," Lydia said. "Now, what was it the two of you wanted to talk to me about?"

CHAPTER TEN

Jeremy exchanged a look with Melanie, and she squeezed his arm in support. It was strange to see the two of them like this, but it was good. She was glad Jeremy had found someone who seemed to fit him so well, even if the happiness he had in his personal life hadn't translated to making him more easygoing at work.

"Well, nothing is certain yet," he said. She could tell from his tone he was trying to put off getting to the point for as long as possible, which was a tactic of his whenever something he needed to say was likely to upset the person he was talking to. "And I've been thinking about this for a while, even before what happened on Saturday."

She wished he would just get to it. She had no clue what he was going to say. Her first thought had been that he and Melanie were getting married, which might have been a bit quick since they had only been in a steady relationship for a few months, but they had dated on and off for years, so it wouldn't have been too surprising.

But it didn't sound like that was what they were here to talk to her about. There was no reason for them to tell her if they were just *thinking* of getting engaged. A knot formed in her stomach. Was Jeremy sick? As much as he got on her nerves, she didn't want him to *die*.

"You're stalling, dear," Melanie said, giving his arm another pointed squeeze. She certainly didn't look upset, so it probably wasn't as bad as Lydia was imagining.

Jeremy took a deep breath. He didn't quite meet her eyes as he spoke. "I'm thinking of leaving the restaurant."

The words were so unexpected, it took her a moment to fully register them. "What?"

"Of leaving Quarry Creek, really," he continued. "I mean, I only moved here for you, and Melanie made me realize how much I miss living in a city. We'd be moving to Chicago, if we were to do this."

"What do you mean you're thinking of leaving the restaurant?"

It was completely out of the blue. If there had been warning signs, she had missed them. Yes, he had been more short tempered than usual at work, but they had all been working themselves to the bone. *Everyone* had been short tempered. As far as she had known, he was just as passionate about Iron and Flame as always.

It reminded her too much of their divorce. Things had been tense between them for a while, and sure, they had hardly seen each other except for in passing since they worked opposite shifts at the restaurant, but she had still been utterly shocked when he sat down with her in the kitchen one evening and said he wanted a divorce.

He grimaced. "Look, it's clear we have different visions for it. Iron and Flame is successful, I'm not going to deny that, but think about it. We're in a small town in the middle of nowhere in Wisconsin. There isn't much more growing we can do. No matter how famous the restaurant gets, people are only going to travel so far for a meal. This town doesn't even have a motel anymore."

"Wausau is half an hour away," she said. "And I heard someone had bought and was planning on renovating that old motel."

"That's the issue. Everyone around here talks like Wausau is a big city. It has, what, forty thousand people? That's nothing compared to somewhere like Chicago. This entire area is so, so … empty. The location is never going to stop holding Iron and Flame back."

"If we grow the restaurant too much, we'll lose what makes it special. There's nothing wrong with keeping it small. We're already almost busier than we can handle. I don't feel like Quarry Creek is holding it back, because I wouldn't want it to be much bigger than this."

"That's what I'm talking about," he said. "We have different visions for the restaurant. I want a lot more than *this*. I want to run a restaurant that's famous around the country. Around the world. Where reservations are made months out instead of hours. And I know there's no guarantee my next restaurant will even make it through the first few years of being open, but if I stay here, then I'm never even going to have a chance to make my vision a reality."

She tried to think. He had blindsided her, and this could change everything, even if they managed to salvage the restaurant's reputation and reopen once the killer was caught.

"What … what would you do with your half of the restaurant?"

"I'd need to sell it, to get the funds that will allow me to open a new one once Melanie and I get settled in Chicago. Our contract states you get first right of refusal if I ever sell my stake in it, but of course I'd offer it to you first anyway." He rubbed the back of his head, looking reluctant to continue. "I'm going to need to sell it for as much as I can. It's not going to be cheap. I'm sorry, but I need the money. I don't want to go deep into debt to open my next restaurant. I've gotten a valuation for my half of Iron and Flame already. I'll email that to you later."

"How long have you been thinking about this?"

"Nearly a year," he admitted. "It was just a passing thought, at first. But the more time I spent thinking of it, and the more I looked into it, the more I realized it might be something I actually wanted to do."

"It sounds like you're pretty certain. You're not just thinking of leaving the restaurant. You're ready to do it."

"Well, I guess, uh… I am. It's going to take us a while to prepare, but we were talking about trying to be settled in a new place in Chicago by the new year."

That was just months away. Lydia felt like the world was spinning around her.

"We need to get a new valuation after all of this settles," she said, her mind racing. "Iron and Flame might not recover from Josh Moore's death. I'm not buying out your half of a failing restaurant."

He grimaced again, but said, "Fair enough."

"You're giving me less than six months, Jeremy," she said. "Really? I have savings, but it's not going to be enough to cover whatever you're asking for your stake in the restaurant. I'll need to get a loan. And how am I supposed to run Iron and Flame by myself?

I'll be the only chef *and* the only owner. I can't do all of both things."

"What about Hank? Maybe he could pick up more shifts—"

"Hank was ready to fully retire before he even started working with us," she snapped. "He's been asking for less work over time, not *more*. Why did you wait until now to say anything? How am I supposed to figure out how to keep the restaurant when we might not even be open again until after you've left?"

"If you can't afford it, I'm sure someone else will be interested in buying out my stake," he said. "They'd help you run it."

She shook her head. That wasn't an option, as far as she was concerned, except as a last resort. There *was* a certain appeal to the thought of having full control and full ownership of Iron and Flame—she just wished it hadn't been sprung on her out of the blue at a time when the restaurant's future was already so uncertain.

"I think getting a new valuation once things settle is fair," Melanie said, glancing between the two of them. "None of us expected this to happen. I know it isn't the best time to tell you, but Jeremy and I discussed it and thought it would be best if everyone was on the same page moving forward, since so much had changed unexpectedly over the weekend."

"I wish you had spoken to me about it sooner," Lydia said to Jeremy. "Just a discussion, letting me know where your mind is at. I don't appreciate being brought into this so late, not when it's something that affects my entire livelihood and my life's passion."

"Well, you know now," he said. "I think I wasn't completely certain of it until Saturday."

"Because of the murder?"

He winced and shook his head. "Spending the shift working side by side with you."

She flinched, hurt. Sure, she had been on the verge of biting his head off for half the shift, but she hadn't decided to up and sell the restaurant because of it. Melanie nudged him, narrowing her eyes, and he quickly explained.

"It made me realize how different we've become over the years and that I would never be able to get *my* vision out there as long as I was tied to this place. Iron and Flame started out as your dream. Me leaving is going to let both of us stretch our wings. I probably should have done it a long time ago."

As much as it stung, and as much as she was going to have to scramble to figure out how to buy out his half of the restaurant and run the place on her own, she knew he was right. Hadn't she just recently been thinking how much easier their divorce would have been with a clean break? Well, here it was, five years late.

"I need some time to myself to think," she said after the silence stretched out too long. "Melanie, it was nice to see you again. Jeremy … we need to get past Josh's murder first. We'll figure everything else out after that. But I do want to purchase your stake in the restaurant. We can straighten the details out later, but don't go looking for another buyer."

She walked them to the door and kept a hand on Saffron's collar in case she decided to try to follow them outside and watched as they got into Jeremy's car. For the second time, he had shaken up her life by telling her he was leaving.

This time, at least she felt better prepared for it.

CHAPTER ELEVEN

The thought of owning and running Iron and Flame on her own was both exhilarating and terrifying. She would be able to make whatever changes she wanted without consulting Jeremy first, but on the other hand, she would be solely responsible for every single issue and stumbling block they hit.

And as things were now, she simply couldn't run the place on her own, even if Hank could be convinced to pick up extra shifts for a while. She would be working twelve-hour days and doing all of the managerial tasks on top of that. She would burn out eventually.

She would either need to hire a business manager or another chef right off the bat. She would probably need both eventually. And she would need to get a loan to buy Jeremy's half of the business, which meant she would have to pay that debt off as quickly as possible.

It would mean a lot of hard work, but now that he had planted the idea in her head, she was becoming more and more eager to make it happen.

All of that was only going to be a possibility if the person who poisoned the risotto was uncovered, though, and even then, it would take time for the restaurant's reputation to recover.

By the time of the staff meeting Wednesday morning, she was at the end of a very frayed rope. Jude had come over both Monday and Tuesday evening and had given her the advice to take it one step at a time, but that was easier said than done. Her mind kept jumping ahead, despite knowing she couldn't plan for anything right now.

She was taking a chance at this staff meeting. If one of her employees wanted her dead badly enough, even the public setting wasn't guaranteed to stop them. It wasn't clear to her whether Jeremy's decision to leave Quarry Creek was a point for or against his innocence, though the fact that nothing had happened during their meeting seemed to be a point for it.

On the one hand, her death would delay and complicate his departure. He had to know she was practically guaranteed to want to buy out his stake in the restaurant, which meant he wouldn't have to spend time looking for another buyer. On the other hand, if he ended up with full ownership of the restaurant before selling it, he could make a lot more money from the sale.

She hated the feeling of having so little trust in him and her employees. She knew this staff meeting might be the last one they had for a long time ... maybe ever. It didn't seem right to go into it with a closed off, wary heart, but one simple fact was inescapable.

The killer was going to be at the park today along with everyone else.

She arrived at the park early enough to set up a cooler of drinks—all sealed cans of soda and unopened bottles of water—and single serving, prepackaged snacks. She didn't want to give the poisoner another chance to strike if she could help it.

There was a lump in her throat as her employees started to arrive. These past few years might not have been perfect, but looking back, they were pretty darn good. She hoped this wasn't the end of the restaurant's story. Even Jeremy looked a little sad as he joined her under the pavilion and made small talk with the employees while they waited for the stragglers to arrive.

Lydia was unsurprised when Mira made a beeline over to him. He looked uncomfortable as soon as she approached. They had gotten sidetracked with his announcement on Monday and hadn't had any time to discuss how he should deal with her. Lydia had hoped he and Melanie would talk about it and figure something out, but it seemed like they hadn't.

Thankfully, the last employee arrived just a couple of minutes later. Jeremy nodded at Lydia when she glanced over at him to see which one of them should start the meeting. He wanted her to do it, and if they were really going to start preparing for her to run the restaurant solo, it made sense that this sort of hands-on announcement should be her job.

It would have been *nice* if he would help, but she had spent enough time agonizing over this meeting that at least she knew what she wanted to say.

She cleared her throat and stepped forward, all eyes turning to her. "Thank you for fitting this meeting into your schedules, everyone," she said. "As many of you know, Iron and Flame was responsible for a man's death Saturday night…"

She explained what happened for the benefit of the people who hadn't been there, careful in her phrasing so that it wouldn't be immediately clear that someone had *murdered* Josh, and it wasn't just some sort of horrible accident. The last thing she needed was for her employees to start hurling accusations at each other here.

"The restaurant is going to be closed indefinitely." She paused as her employees groaned. Gabe swore out loud, only to flush and look away with a muttered apology when she looked at him with raised eyebrows. Penny frowned at him too. The two of them were standing close together but not holding hands. It seemed they still wanted to keep their relationship quiet. "Sorry, I know that's not what anyone wanted to hear. Until we know more about what happened, I think reopening the restaurant is too risky. We can't take the chance that someone else will get hurt. I wish I had better news. All I can promise is that I'll be in touch as soon as I know what Iron and Flame's future looks like."

She and Jeremy had exchanged a few emails earlier this morning and had agreed not to mention the fact that he might be stepping away from the restaurant until they knew more. Unlike Iron and Flame's closure, it wouldn't directly affect the employees—well, other than Mira—and everything was too up in the air right now anyway.

"I think we can all read between the lines," Gabe called out. "Are you saying the restaurant might never reopen? You're going out of business?"

Chatter broke out amongst the group. Lydia had to raise her voice to get them to quiet again.

"None of us want to see the restaurant's doors close forever," she said. "But I don't want to make promises I might not be able to keep. Yes, there is a chance that this is it for Iron and Flame. Jeremy and I will be available to answer any questions you have. Feel free to mingle for a while; we'll stay until everyone's gone."

She sat down at one of the picnic tables with a sigh. That could have gone better, she supposed, but it also could have gone worse.

"Hey, Melanie lent me her camera, she said we should find someone to take a group picture of all of us," Jeremy said as he approached her. "I left it in my car. Mind holding down the fort while I go get it?"

She nodded and waved him off. It was nice of Melanie to think of that, even if it made the whole thing feel that much more final.

Frowning, she watched as Mira peeled away from the group to follow Jeremy back toward the parking lot, but he would have to handle her on his own, because Chartreuse was approaching her with a worried expression on her face.

"Do you really think the restaurant will close?" she asked. "Should we start looking for new jobs?"

"I wish I could tell you, but I just don't know. I hope we can reopen and work hard to get close to where we were before this weekend. But I understand the staff needs to make ends meet. I don't want to ask anyone to put off finding a new job while we wait to find out what's going to happen to the restaurant."

"I'm not going to find another job this good in Quarry Creek," her sous chef said. "I'm just not. Iron and Flame was supposed to be a career for me. There isn't another restaurant like it in the area."

Lydia considered Chartreuse for a long moment. The younger woman had been on the staff as a sous chef for a long time—since before her and Jeremy's divorce, even. She was skilled in the kitchen, a reliable employee, and knew the restaurant like the back of her hand.

She also hadn't been working Saturday night, so there was absolutely no way she was behind the poisoning incident.

If Jeremy went ahead with leaving, they would need at least one more head chef on roster, someone to oversee the shifts Lydia wasn't working. Lydia realized that chef had been right under her nose the whole time. Chartreuse wasn't the inexperienced young cook she had been when they hired her anymore, and she hadn't been for a long time. She didn't have to worry about hiring another chef, because she already had one.

"I can't promise anything," Lydia said slowly. "But no one wants to see the restaurant close less than I do.

I'm going to fight tooth and nail for it. If you can hold out for a couple of weeks while we figure out what's going on and what's going to happen next, I'd like to schedule a meeting with you to discuss your career going forward."

"Should I be excited or worried?"

Lydia smiled. "Excited."

Chartreuse grinned at her. "I think I can wait a couple of weeks, then."

"Excuse me," Jaelin said as she came over to join them. "Lydia, Penny, and Gabe are having an argument, and Penny seems pretty upset. I don't know what's going on, but it seems like the sort of thing you might need to handle."

"Where are they?" she asked.

"Over behind that building with the restrooms. I was heading over there to use the ladies' room when I heard them. I think she was crying."

Lydia winced. "Right. I'll go see what's up. Jeremy should be back soon, and he's going to want to do a group picture, so try to start getting people ready for that."

She rose from her seat and headed toward the restrooms, worried about Penny. It had been an emotional morning so far, but she hadn't forgotten that there was a killer here. She just hoped she wasn't walking into a trap.

CHAPTER TWELVE

She heard the argument before she even reached the building. Penny's voice was raised, and judging from the quaver in her words, Jaelin had been right when she said the other woman was crying.

"I know you're lying! Just tell me the truth!"

Lydia paused. If this was a personal argument, maybe she *shouldn't* get involved. Yes, they were at a work event, but it wasn't exactly a formal one. This sounded like it was about their relationship, which was exactly none of her business.

She couldn't make out Gabe's response, but she could hear Penny's reply, because it was an inarticulate sound of grief.

She sounded distraught. Lydia wavered for another moment, then decided that she should at least go make sure everything was all right. She rounded the corner of the bathroom building just in time to see Gabe grab Penny and pull her into a hug.

Penny started to sob into his shoulder. Lydia began backing away, deciding that this was clearly a very private moment, and as long as no one was getting hurt, she wasn't needed here. Then Penny opened her eyes and saw her. Her face went pale, but her expression firmed as she pulled away from her boyfriend.

"Lydia's here, Gabe."

Gabe's shoulders tensed. Slowly, he turned around to face her. He only glanced at her for a second before turning his head to look at Penny. She held his gaze for a long moment, then squared her shoulders and faced Lydia.

"Gabe has something to tell you."

"What's going on?" she asked.

"I'm quitting," he said.

"Gabe!" Penny elbowed him.

STEAK IT OR LEAVE IT

Lydia hesitated, looking between them. That obviously hadn't been what he was supposed to say. But what could *Gabe* possibly have to tell her that was so important.

Unless ... he was behind the murder. She had known he was a suspect. Everyone who was there that night was, even Jeremy. But out of all of them, Gabe seemed to have the least motive of anyone. He had no reason to want *her* out of the picture, and his connection to Josh Moore was tenuous at best.

But he and Penny clearly cared about each other. They might have been keeping their relationship quiet while at work, but Lydia could tell just by looking at them that they were in love. Was getting revenge on someone who had wronged a loved one a strong enough motive for an otherwise normal young man to commit murder?

He'd had the opportunity. He was the last person to stir the risotto, other than her, and he hadn't taken over until after Mira had already gotten all of the cleaning supplies out of the cupboard. He could have snagged one of the cans and sprayed the oven cleaner into the pot of risotto in a matter of seconds.

She swallowed, her blood suddenly running cold.

"It was you, wasn't it?"

For a second, Gabe looked like he was about to panic, but Penny grabbed his hand and squeezed it. He took a deep breath.

"Yeah. It was. I'm sorry."

Penny's lips trembled, and she wiped tears away from her eyes. "I had a sneaking suspicion that kept growing over these past few days, but I thought I was going crazy. How could I think my *boyfriend* would do something like that? It wasn't until I saw how upset he was when you announced that the restaurant might close that I knew my suspicions were right. He didn't just look upset. He looked guilty."

Lydia closed her eyes. She took a deep breath and let it out slowly while she gathered her thoughts. Horror and confusion filled her to the brim, but there was enough space left over for another, more selfish emotion.

Relief.

If Gabe confessed, they might have a chance of saving the restaurant.

"Why?" she asked. "I just... I don't understand. Who were you even trying to hurt? I almost ate that risotto, Gabe. I almost *died.*"

"I had no idea you made enough for yourself too, I swear," he said, almost stumbling over his words in a rush to get them out. "I thought the order was just for Mr. Moore. If I'd thought anyone else might eat any of it, I never would have done what I did."

"Even if that's true, you still committed *murder.* I don't get it. You're a smart and hardworking young man with a lovely girlfriend, a job that, if you'll excuse me for tooting my own horn, is pretty decent, and your whole future ahead of you. Why throw all of that away?"

"He did it for me," Penny said, her voice wobbling. "He knew about Mr. Moore before he came to eat at the restaurant. I worked for him for a year as his secretary, and it was the worst year of my life. I cried when I got home from work every day. He was a cruel pig. He made all sorts of comments about my body and my hair and what I was wearing. He belittled me in front of his clients. He called me stupid if I had to ask a question. He was bad enough that I still doubt my self-worth to this day." She sniffed. "Seeing him on Saturday brought it all back."

Gabe tried to pull her into a hug, but she pushed him away, and he relented, looking hurt. "When I saw how strongly she reacted just to seeing him, something in me snapped," he admitted. "I was doing all I could not to go out there and punch him. When I saw those cleaners on the counter and I was left to stir the risotto while everyone else was busy, I just grabbed one on impulse and sprayed it into the food. I wasn't even thinking far enough ahead to think that it might kill him. I just wanted to hurt him any way I could. It was a mistake. I know that. I've known that since the second I set the plate down in front of him. I didn't mean to kill him, or to almost poison you, or to make the restaurant close down, or any of this. I'd give anything to go back in time and change it all."

Penny had to wipe her tears away again, but she moved away from his side to stand by Lydia. "I can't be with you anymore, Gabe," she whispered. "I'm sorry."

Lydia had to blink away tears of her own. One impulse had destroyed so much.

"I know," Gabe replied. "It's okay. I'm sorry too. I love you, Penny. I'll wait here while you guys call the police. I know I can't make this right, but I'm going to spend the rest of my life trying."

EPILOGUE

"Here's to your first weekend back at work." Jude touched his wine glass to hers in a toast, and Lydia took a sip of her wine, smiling.

"Thanks. It was hectic, but we did a lot better than I'd dared to hope."

"I have complete faith that Iron and Flame is going to end up being just fine," he said. "Have you announced that Jeremy's leaving yet?"

She shook her head and paused to pat the couch next to her to invite Saffron up before she responded. "Not yet. I want to wait until we do a new valuation and I have the loan approval. I don't want to announce anything until it's certain."

"You'll get it," he said with a grin. "You're finally going to have full creative freedom at the restaurant."

A shiver of anticipation went through her as she thought of the possibilities. "I don't want to jinx it, but I really hope you're right. These next few months are going to be more stressful than ever, though. We need to do a lot just to recover from Josh's death and the publicity surrounding Gabe's confession, and on top of that, I need to figure out how to structure the business going forward."

"You need to take time for yourself too," he said. "I think you should take some time while Jeremy's still here and you *can* take the time off."

She sipped her wine as she considered. "You're right, I guess this might be my last chance for a vacation for a long time. I can talk to Jeremy about it. He owes me that much, at least. What do you think we should do?"

He smiled. "It's your vacation. You should choose. I'm happy with anything as long as we're together. Saffron can always stay at a doggy daycare if it's not something she can join us for."

Saffron's tail thumped against the couch at the sound of her name, and Lydia stroked the top of her head.

"No, she should come with us." She thought for a few minutes, then said, "A camping trip might be fun. It's the very beginning of fall, so it shouldn't be too cold or too hot. We could invite some friends, find a nice campsite with plenty of amenities to enjoy, and just kick back for a couple of days."

"You are a woman after my heart," he said, leaning over to kiss her.

Lydia felt a warm glow. She still had a lot to figure out, and the future was never certain. Jeremy had had his own little adventure while she was dealing with Gabe and Penny; when Mira followed him to his car, she tried to kiss him after confessing her feelings, and he had fired her on the spot. He hadn't even *told* Lydia until a few days later, but she supposed in all of the other excitement, she could understand how the news might have gotten lost in the shuffle.

Still, it meant that between Gabe's arrest and Mira's firing, they were short-staffed at the restaurant—even more so now that she wanted to start training Chartreuse to take over Jeremy's role as the restaurant's second head chef. She and Jeremy had to figure out the details of her taking over his stake in the restaurant, and they needed to work hard to help the restaurant's reputation recover.

But she had time for a vacation. A nice, relaxing camping trip with her boyfriend and his dog and a couple of their friends. She was looking forward to having a couple of stress-free days for once in her life and could hardly wait to get their trip planned and booked.

All she needed was one week where nothing went wrong.